Hiwholthin
by Paul E. Shinkle

Also by Paul E Shinkle

23: Stories Short

Hiwholthin: A Supernatural Love

For MS,

Who has, intuitively, always known Leo.

The author gratefully acknowledges the educators and researchers at The Abraham Lincolns Classroom for the fair use Lincoln quote used in this work of fiction.

The author expresses respect and heartfelt appreciation the beta readers and most especially his Editor, Jinx Moreland, for their most fruitful critiques.

Most of all, he tips a well-worn hat to the women and men who operate movable bridges across the United States. It is difficult and sometimes dangerous work. Bridge operations guarantee someone, either on land or on water (usually both), will be aggravated because the bridge is either down or up. Every Bridge Operator knows and lives is the reality that the purpose of a bridge is to bring people together.

One way or another.

Foreword

The earliest movable bridge over the Milwaukee River connected the east and west sides of Wisconsin Avenue. It was a swing bridge. A swing bridge is held in place at the far side by locks that keep the movable part solidly against terra firma. The near side is rooted on a capstan, a rotating gear. Before electricity, the capstan at the Wisconsin Avenue swing bridge moved thanks to Eldred, a sturdy workhorse too old to plow.

Eldred's Bridge Operator was a salty old geezer almost 43 years old, a sturdy workhorse in his own way, a veteran of the Civil War, with a bad hip (musket ball), a penchant for bourbon (strictly medicinal), and a love of Walt Whitman.

The Bridge Operator's name was Leo. History claims no last name for him. Leo was not at all shy about shaking down a passing wagon for a bucket of oats for Eldred, a dozen eggs for his own lunch, or a snort of medicine for his hip. He would reject even a polite refusal and have Eldred sit down, thereby holding the bridge span open indefinitely, as wagons stacked up waiting to cross the Milwaukee River.

They could sit there, by God, until hell froze over, which potential was more or less constantly imminent in Wisconsin.

He and Eldred did all right for themselves.

Eldred grew to love listening to Leo read "Leaves of Grass" as he walked the big circle, pulling the Wisconsin Avenue Swing Bridge open and closed, allowing sailing vessels, tugs, and barges to go upriver and downriver, from and to Lake Michigan, flowing between the city's stinking streets where the tanneries, foundries, and outhouses fouled air, land, and water with chemicals, carcasses, and humanure.

Sometimes, Leo recited from memory a bit of a speech from Abraham Lincoln, given not far from their bridge, decades ago. Abe said, "To correct the evils, great and small, which spring from want of sympathy, and from positive enmity, among strangers, as nations, or as individuals, is one of the highest functions of civilization."

"That's what a bridge is, Eldred. A highest function of civilization."

Leo finally died one day, at work, and therefore happy. Eldred was retired to pasture where he lived another decade, alternately walking around in a circle, or sitting down until he got some oats, and always looking for his beloved Operator.

The wonder of electricity made Eldred obsolete but not the Bridge Operators. They learned to push the movable spans open and closed with electric motors, eventually operating the new safety gates and bells that, when the bridge was open to the boats, kept most of the ordinary drunks, the foolishly curious, or tragically inattentive others from walking into open space and, immediately thereafter, into the fetid Milwaukee River.

Although their skillset changed over the decades, Bridge Operators' attitudes about land, people, booze, and hard work largely did not. By the time this story begins, they were still tough as hell, men and women, with interests in fine arts, music, philosophy, crafts, and astronomy that belied their blue-collar labor, and with an unusually healthy appreciation for the benefits of a bit of medicine to loosen up their joints and their attitudes, as the river forever flowed beneath their feet and their aching hips.

A modern Bridgehouse is typically three stories high. At the river level, are the motors and mechanicals, their watertight pits dipping another 20 feet below the river's surface, allowing the massive counterweights to move in their controlled falling and rising.

The middle level of a Bridgehouse is a combination of high-voltage electrical boxes, each bigger than a closet, a couple of salvaged school lockers for the workers to share, and a very basic bathroom.

The topmost level houses a rugged control panel or two, festooned with a dozen multi-colored status indicator lights, levers, touch screens, and the tattered detritus of outdated sticky notes. These told the history of the mechanical snafus, workarounds, incantations, and curses necessary to make the neglected infrastructure function.

There was usually, not always, a salvaged but comfortable chair, a thrift store mini-frig and microwave, and a desk no fewer than 40 years old, full of relevant, irrelevant, and irreverent paperwork and magazines, plus a dozen pens, most of which were spent or dried up.

These contemporary Bridge Operators continued old Leo's work traditions. They sassed anyone they damn chose to and for whatever reason suited them. They would just as passionately run to help a pedestrian who fell on their bridge as a drunk who fell off one. They answered, without audible complaint, several hundred times a year the difference between a bascule bridge (two movable leaves that part in the middle), a lift bridge (a single movable section moves straight up and down), and drawbridges which, by definition, all moveable bridges are, not only the ones found at castles, for God's sake, how dumb can you be? All draw bridges move so that boats in the water below them, called the draw, can pass. And to hell with cars, buses, horses, and pedestrians.

They were the toughest romantics you could imagine.

Chapter 1:

The *Thiflessa*

Strong stirring inside woke her.

Body still, her eyes check every edge. She feels into her safe space, her *thiflessa*. No threats. Good space.

Safe. Unseen. Unknown.

The light has shifted since yesterday. Lower, earlier, darker shadows. Better hunting.

She moves her head slowly, just far enough to push under the water's surface, peering past the edge of the entrance to the *thiflessa* into the river beyond. Her clear lids—her *wessethia*—smooth over porraceous eyes. Everything about her moves smoothly. Like water, like light.

Like alert intelligence.

Fallen leaves ooze downward, drifting in spirals from the river's surface toward its bottom muck. Flickers of food there and there. There. The underside of a fat loon preparing to dive. Enticed, she pauses, feeling its hunger.

Feeling her own.

Darker soon. Better.

She moves back into the *thiflessa* as if liquid, stretching her arms, hands flowing over her breasts, her face, above her head. Pushing fully, she presses hard against the mossy back wall, enjoying her own strength. She uncurls her legs, spins around, and dips her feet into the river's water just beyond.

Safe here. Good *thiflessa*.

She grooms small bones from her hair, tossing bits of dry things to the side, licking fish scales off the exquisitely sensitive skin between her fingers. She is hungry.

Not only for food.

A strong urge to plan but no urgency to act. She allows the tension. There is time. The stirring inside thrills her. She reaches into the river and cups handfuls of water against her belly, water colder today than yesterday. Good flow.

Time to hunt. Move now.

She slips into the river. No ripple, no sound.

Chapter 2:

The Tender Bridge Tender

Leo Milhoan stepped onto the river-level pitwalk under the Wisconsin Avenue lift bridge, twenty-three feet below the road deck overhead. He glanced to his left, downward a further twenty feet to the bottom of the cement-walled counterweight pit, which opened just past the inside safety rail.

Then he turned to his right, faced the Milwaukee River.

His River.

As smooth as black ink tonight, it suffered no reflection. Utterly still at the surface, grudgingly absorbing the splash from the amber street lights, shaking off the smudge of the five red navigation lights on the bridge support piers, ignoring the silver sliver of half-moon trying to shimmer here and there.

He lit a cigarette. Dropped it immediately. Scrunched it underfoot.

"To hell with that," he susurrated to his River, matching his voice to Her soft surface.

"I gotta quit. Ain't getting any younger, too bad. Keep smoking, I ain't gonna get much older."

His gaze drifted a block upriver, toward the Wells Street bridge. He noted a bit of an eddy swirling past its support piers. His River was forever untamed, flowing as She wished, intensely mysterious. The water roiled around Wells, defying the surrounding black glass surface, as She desired, responding to who the hell knew what—or who—might lay there on Her bed.

The tour boat captains nicknamed this stretch "The Canyon," where they often found their apartment-building-sized vessels suddenly pushed diagonally toward the concrete seawalls by wind and current at the exact moment they needed to be dead straight on in order to clear the draw, that precious width of water just broad enough a gap to sail safely between the unforgiving concrete buttresses of the bridge support piers.

Tonight, besides the strange roiling just south of the Wells Street draw, She was flat black at the surface, brooding with a victim-seeking malevolence.

He acknowledged Her hunger.

"Keep to your ways, Love," he whispered. "I'll keep to mine."

He moved downriver along the narrow pitwalk, toward the Michigan Street bridge. Another eddy there, this one more melancholy, indecisive, curious.

Muddled by all the possible ways She *could* take a life, pulling a craft under, dashing a Captain's hubris against the relentlessly confining seawalls on both of Her sides, sweet-talking the aggressive drunk who dared piss into Her face to merely step off the hard edge into blessed peace, She had nevertheless managed to kill no one this season.

Yet.

"You'll get a dozen at once, one night," he said to Her gently. "You have before. Please Love, not tonight."

Nothing tobacco to do with his hands, he put a worn boot up against the riverside safety railing and leaned forward. Something, maybe a fish, a big one, splashed downriver.

He appreciated the ripples as they bounced asymmetrically off the far seawall, then back again, weaving through themselves toward him. He appreciated the tiny flecks of moonlight on their little tops.

Milhoan slipped his old uncle's stainless-steel flask out of a hip pocket. A wee snort of Scotch to take the edge off the early autumn wind.

It was a fine single malt, smooth and warming. He did not drink cheap. Not a wise practice to drink at all when at work, he thought, as he usually did. But it was the best way he knew to stave off the twin fiends of clear memories of long-past love and the pressing loneliness usually at hand.

"Better'n nuthin," he said.

Smoky. Peaty. The wet fire went to his core and lifted his mood.

"You're a great River. On a Great Lake. A toast to your Royal Riverness," he raised the flask to Her and enjoyed another, heartier, swallow. Then, following precisely his self-authored ritual guidebook, he offered Her three—just three—drops.

Chapter 3:

She Sees: *Flissanthia!*

A week later, Milhoan leaned against the concrete wall along the pitwalk, looking at the water.

"Hello, River," he said softly. "This will be a long night. A long night in a short life."

Five hours earlier, Doctor Rob Schafhirt leaned across his desk.

"Leo, we have made so many advances in medicine in so many disease processes during my 30 years in practice. Your case is a bit of an outlier. Good advances in care and remission. Solid advances, to be sure. Far better outcomes than even a decade ago."

Schafhirt paused. His patient notes tablet cast blue anxiety onto his cheeks and forehead.

"But still not great. Not even good enough. My heart begs me to lie to you. My God, Leo. We've known each other since I started this practice."

I figured bad news was coming, Milhoan thought. But this is a blow I wasn't ready for. I gotta help Rob through this.

"Your rookie year, Doc. Your prices were good. But you sucked as a physician." Milhoan winked at him, curling his fingers to keep them from trembling.

"Beggars can't be choosers—for either of us," Schafhirt snickered. "As I recall, you stiffed me on the bill."

"I did indeed," Milhoan laughed. "I was flat-assed broke at the time. I also recall, thanks for not mentioning my generous heart for hell's sake, that I paid you later with a very fine bottle of single malt."

"Best Speyside I ever had, no doubt."

Schafhirt looked at the screen again, imploring it to update data with a miracle link ready to download.

"Leo, it's time to get very serious. And from now on, no more 'Doc.' Got it? Unless you want me to start calling you Bridge Tender First Class Milhoan, dammit."

Milhoan laughed. "Please, please. It is Senior Bridge Tender First Class."

He paused, took a deeper breath than he intended to.

"Okay, Rob. I'm set for the worst. Say it all now and fast. Then we'll make plans."

"If we start treatment tomorrow, this week at the latest, then it's fair to say you'll have a year, as many as two. Including the time it'll take to recover from surgery," he said. "It's fast growing; often treatable, but we've found it late.

"It's frontal lobe. Left untreated, expect rapid shifts between you at your considerable brightest and best—and progressively severe cognitive difficulties, including the possibility of hallucinations.

"Post-op, it's likely that you'll not be healthy enough to return to work. Ever."

Milhoan scanned his face for even false hope. He found none.

Harder for Rob than for me, Leo thought. I better help him get this over with. He's only got that one thing to say.

"Thanks for not lying to me, Rob. 'As many as' ain't all that encouraging. My work is damn near my whole life. Work and the nephew. You know that.

"You've cross-checked everything, right? No chance of another smashingly handsome Leo Milhoan in the system who's supposed to be getting bad news instead of me."

Schafhirt looked up.

"I would love to lie to you, Leo. Damn it all, I even thought about it, to hell with medical ethics. Send you on your way with some Socratic Noble Lie until you came back in two seasons, too sick to even treat. I might have done that with a lesser man.

"But you're the toughest bastard I have ever known. You are more alive than any patient I've ever treated. Probably why the Scotch and smokes didn't kill you earlier."

"I'm flattered that you remember our work together on Socrates. You Docs are bright as hell, but too narrowly focused.

"I did quit smoking, Rob. Toldja I would. Don't suppose that gets me any bonus time."

"You quit on your first try, too. Do you know how rare a thing that is?

"Don't think I'm being brave, Leo. I wanted to lie to you. But I knew that if I had, you'd have personally kicked my ass from your deathbed."

Milhoan laughed hard. "Gimme some credit, Rob. I would have hired some pros to pound you."

"I'm sure you would have."

They each looked anywhere that was not at the other.

I guess we only ever have today, Milhoan thought. Steady now. Don't make it hard on Rob. Cover up. Make it easy for him.

"Seriously, Leo I won't lie to patients. I would never lie to you, even if I thought it would be better for you."

"Thanks for that, Rob. By the gods, I cannot abide a liar."

"Nor can I, my old friend. Nor can I."

They looked away from each other, sharing the clear office window, facing an early setting autumn sun, slipping away behind sagging golden trees.

Schafhirt pulled another tissue. Handed the box across the desk.

"Damn you, Leo." He covered his face.

"Love you more, Rob," Leo said and covered his own.

An hour later, a palliative care plan featuring Scotch and honesty stood completed, they shook hands.

"What are you going to do today, Leo?"

"I'm going to work, Rob. A double. A full load of vessels to get through the bridge until midnight, then on standby for emergencies until 6 tomorrow morning. Got an Edenkoben cuckoo clock to finish restoring with my nephew for his birthday. That kid's a gem. He wanted me to find a broken one to teach him on. We'll have time enough for that.

"There's always time for love."

"If you can find it," Schafhirt said.

"That's the damn catch, Rob, ain'a? Looks like I'm not going to waste time trying to find any more of it. The kid, the clock, and my River are enough for me. They have to be."

He put his hands in his pockets and jingled his keys.

"OK, I'll keep in touch. Let's tie one on pretty soon, my friend. Hate to get on the far side without hearing your drunken zither playing again."

"For your goddam information, I'm the best zither player you'll ever meet."

"Thank God you're the only zither player I'll ever meet."

They laughed. Embraced for a long time.

"Get the hell out of my office, ya bum," he said.

"Doctor's orders, right?"

The door closed.

"Gonna hurt me more than you," Rob said quietly through the door.

"Hey, Nora. Please cancel my afternoon patients. If anything urgent comes up, please ship it over to Dr. Sally. I'll call her now."

"Very well, Doctor. Are you okay?"

"No, Nora. I'm not okay at all. I appreciate you asking, though. I will see you tomorrow morning."

Hours later, darkness rooted around Milhoan, closing him into the timeless night.

He turned the outside safety lights off as soon as he cleared the steel Bridgehouse door. The pitwalk was very dark. Even the night bugs abandoned him for streetlights above and beyond his sight.

Outside and under the bridge, he leaned against the cement wall behind him, one foot on the steel safety railing in front of him. He stared at his River. The stainless-steel hip flask was in his hand before he sought it.

He took a sip, maybe three.

The River, his River, so beautiful at night. Tears brimmed and he sipped again. She-river who never rejected or judged.

The River begged to claim him. She called to him, the invitation he always declined, "Come to your peace with Me."

"Not tonight, Love," he said as always. "Maybe tomorrow. Just not tonight."

He turned to the railing by the counterweight pit, his back now to the River. Urinated into the pit, never ever into the River.

"No offense," he said over his shoulder to his River-lover.

"None was taken," She said. "Come in. Everything is fine in me. You will be forever loved here."

"Maybe tomorrow," he whispered. "Not tonight."

He zipped up and popped a squeeze of hand sanitizer into his palm.

Motion to his left caught his eye. He slowly turned toward it. Don't react too fast, he thought. Let it come into view.

She sat on the edge of a construction barge downriver, grooming herself, stretching discretely in the dim quarter-moon light, her feet in the water, pulling the fur from an earlier kill off her hands.

Milhoan gawked through the dripping darkness. Fast clouds crossed the face of the moon.

"Jesus. I need a little Scottish courage." He tipped the flask butt up to the heedlessly clouding indigo sky.

She paused her tidying up to look at him, keen eyes curious about the silver flicker in his hands.

There shouldn't be anyone over there, he thought. Probably another drunk fell off the pier onto that barge. Lucky dunce. I might have to radio the Coast Guard for a rescue.

"Hey there!" He cupped his hands around his mouth. "Do you need help?"

Her instincts surged. She froze, one hand near her mouth, the other on her belly. Perfectly still.

"Do you need rescuing? Help of any kind? Are you okay?"

She seethed silently. Seen by an Other. She was furious. *Flissanthia!* Be invisible in plain sight! That is the creed of her kind.

Kill it, her next thought.

Kill it before it can go to others. Kill it and feed. Protect the *Elowinithin*, the baby within. Feed the *Elowinithin*. Kill it. It has seen me.

She scanned, motionless, eyes only. Are there others? Or *Sha-sha*, just one, just this one? She watches as it shifted forward, trying to make sense of what it is seeing. She snarls softly, as much at herself as at this Other.

She locks onto it.

"I can see you there. Hey!" Milhoan called out. "Are you hurt? Are you drunk?"

She feels into its voice. He is a One-Safe, she decides. *Eh'blemanthon*. Safe. Friend.

Riskless. Riskless? No. It is dangerous, but not right now. And not to me.

Khakhathontha. Not now dangerous; later dangerous. *Khakhathontha*. No need to kill. Yet. It sees me as one of its kind, she thought. It is air-dependent. Prey-like.

Manessimuna. Food. Or a killer.

If I flee in silence, she thinks, will it chase? If I flee with *shessishess*, splashing noise, will it chase?

Move. Now.

She *shessishess* into the water, making as much noise as possible, and moves swiftly away.

On the pitwalk, Milhoan watched as she disappeared. "No drunk swims like that or dives like that. What the hell is going on? Rob said I'd get goofy. Later, near the end. Am I losing my shit already or what?"

He moved to the Bridgehouse door, ready to head up to the Operator's level. His breath felt harsh, his palms wet with sweat, and a tremble in his legs.

He paused. Looked at where she was moments ago.

"My, God," he said to the River. "Whatever that was, it was beautiful."

Downriver, she crested the edge of wet and air and watched him go inside. She watched still, feeling the stirring of her *Elowinithin*, her baby. But nothing for the next, her Second?

She felt the keening urgency to flow the second *Elowinithin*. True to her kind she was *thipthipetha*, evolved to express concurrent gestations. Two uteri. She needed a second baby inside her. Now. A Second to carry the line forward.

She stares at the place where he had been.

Urgency. *Halawanthala*. For her Second. For the line.

For him.

A half a block further downriver, this time utterly silently, she dives deeply, pushing herself and her one baby back upriver toward their den, back toward it, until she was safe inside her *thiflessa*.

She lay there, shaking water off her rich fur. Safe now. Still, but alert. Ready to kill it if it pursues. It is *Manessimuna*—equal prey and predator. She is still hungry, but wary.

And very, very curious.

Chapter 4

Urgency *Halawanthala*

She awakens agitated.

Growls. Everything last night was *khakhath'ontha*, dangerous later. Onrushing danger. Her *thiflessla* suddenly feels cramped. She needs to move.

Her face is underwater now. No *manessimuma*, no food now. Too much light now.

She pulls back and touches her belly. Feels life. *Sha-sha*. Only one life, not two. She has become a *thiflessa*.

But with an empty room for another. She is *thipthipen*. Two-bearing. She must bear two. The weight of the continuance of her kind, the exigency of her fertile season pushes against her agitation.

There is little time. Food. For her, for the baby, her *Elowininthin*. What of that Other? *Eh'blemanthon*, Mate-love? Or *Manessimuma*? Feed on it?

Both?

The Other cannot *shelossithis*—it cannot swim without effort. It is defective.

Manessimuma then? Feed on it? Or not? How can it join with her if it cannot *shelossithis*? It will die in the water.

Without the Other, she will *sha-sha*, just one. Eventually, her kind, the Afleni, will die out. Each *Elowininthin* must have a Second, a next. No generation can stand alone. She knows she will die one day, but there must be One and One More before she can pass.

One and One More of the *Aflenis*, the Water Cleavers, One beyond the wee one she caresses through herself.

Whether *Eh'blemanthon*, *Khakhatontha*, or *Manessimuma*, she must try to Second. She can find no other *Afleni* to mate with.

It is too light to hunt. She is impatient, yet must wait. She must *shesmen'athuma*, mate-love with it soon. Touch it. Take it. Push it into. Mate it. Withdraw life with it.

Project new life with it. Maybe kill and feed on it for her *Elowinithin*. Both of them, if she can Second.

She growls impatiently.

Soon.

Chapter 5:

Time Tick

Leo Milhoan washed and carefully dried his hands at the sink one level down from the Bridge Operator's Level. Glanced at the tired man in the mirror.

"Ain't done yet, ya old bastard," he nodded respectfully. "Ain't dead yet either. At least this thing won't hurt. Much. Or long."

He noticed tears stinging his eyes.

"To hell with that. There's a clock to fix. It has no time to give. And I have none to spare."

Back at the top level of the Bridgehouse, he lifted a pristine, walnut box from his ratty backpack and laid his handcrafted sisal tool pouch gently to the side.

He expected to find its inner works a surly mess of disrepair. It was never intended to be a museum piece. But it was an extraordinary and rare clock nonetheless. Now it would connect him forever to his only nephew, Ed. If he lived long enough for them to finish restoring it together.

He had found the cuckoo clock years before in a small shop near an austere hostel in Edenkoben, a pass-by village in southern Germany. Neglected, but beautiful.

The shop was small, probably intended as a guard shack for tax collectors when it was built in the 1600s. Thick walled, tiny windowed. Warm and safe. It might have felt oppressive without the dozens of classic cuckoos ticking and tocking on every square meter of the interior. The two proprietors lived on the second floor, no doubt a cozy, warm hideaway with exactly one extraordinary clock, never shared with mere customers.

"Certainly, the gentleman would prefer restoring a time piece that is more readily a gift, *nicht wahr*?" The German shopkeeper cast a baleful eye between Milhoan and the clock that fixed his attention.

"You are very kind to note the state of this exceptional piece, *Mein Herr*," he said. "I am grateful for your candor. And for you permitting me to visit your extraordinary store. I stand humbled and enchanted."

"*Danke Schön,* Herr Milhoan."

The clock's housewood was in very good condition. The face carved from precious ebony, not plastic, *natürlich*. Its hands and numbers were of ivory. The number 3 was missing its connecting swirl, otherwise, the exterior was in near-fine condition.

"It is my intention to restore it, Herr Schuller. I harbor a deep commitment to bringing it to life again. *Aber*, I must disclose to you, that I intend to take it home to Milwaukee with me, work on it there and apprentice my young nephew at the same time. So, it will be lost to *Deutschland* if you sell it to me. However, it will be restored and cherished."

"*Eine Augenblick*, Herr Milhoan. I must consult with my wife. *Bitte*, look at other less challenging pieces until I return."

Milhoan made a show of looking at the inventory, each of the other timepieces remarkable in some way. Always making sure he was within earshot of their conversation.

"*Nein*, Tomas," he heard Frau Schuller say. "*Das ist nicht ordnung.*"

"Come, meet him, my dear. There is an authenticity about him. Although his German is poor," he said. Gently and firmly at the same time.

Milhoan smiled out the window. The street straddled the centuries, stern-faced locals on task and dazzled tourists turning their heads greedily. It was cloudy and rain-threatened this morning, but the entire tableau was crisply efficient. The interior of the shop was all brown study, enough but not too much light, with a museum feel, and a perfectly tidy, timeless space for the timepieces. Two protective, brooding shopkeeps.

My *Deutschkenntnisse* is not so poor as you think, Herr Schuller. Nor am I nearly as out of order as *deine Frau* believes, either.

"*Guten Tag*," she folded her hands at her waist.

She wore a crisp worker's apron over her business dress. She was a clock worker, too. Milhoan paused before speaking. She loved, quite clearly, every clock in the store. The thought of one leaving Germany was as inconceivable as a neighbor setting off one languid afternoon in the dead of winter a hundred and fifty years ago, finally tired of endless wars to go live in America.

She looked at him with equal parts robust skepticism and intelligent curiosity. If she also saw him as a skilled clock worker, he thought, things might go better.

"*Guten Tag*, Frau Schuller. *Wie geht es Ihnen*?"

"I am well today, Herr Milhoan," she said firmly in English. "Thank you."

She managed to assay him to the bone with a quick scan up and down.

"Yours is not a German name. But this is a German clock. I know you will appreciate our temerity in considering its sale. Edenkoben is a small place, an eddy between a thousand years of war and far too little peace, much of that more recent than we would have hoped for. We are, I'm sure you will appreciate, loathe to lose the artifacts of our cultural heritage. At least if the clock is in Germany, we can seek to reacquire it were its placement to become unsuitable."

"Temerity," Milhoan smiled softly inside. Her English is far better than I thought. Far better than my German.

"Milhoan was my father's name, Frau Schuller. My mother's maiden name was Kaltenborn. Her mother's name was Schenkel. And her father's name was Elknisch."

She gasped sharply.

"*Welcher nahmen*? What name did you say?"

"Yes, Frau Schuller. Elknisch. My great-grandfather was Heinrich Elknisch. The same name that I trust we will find inscribed in his own hand inside this clock, on the floor of the structure, on the 3 o'clock side. My given name is indeed Milhoan. But my blood, and my love of this craft, is Elknisch. I would not be so indiscreet as to suggest I am an Edenkobener. But I must confess that my blood feels quite settled being here with you and Herr Schuller."

He paused.

"Irrespective of what you may permit of this piece, this experience, please do trust, this is certainly not primarily a transaction. It is an affirmation of relation."

She glanced at his hands. Too rough, perhaps. But he holds them with elegance.

"But have you the skill, Herr Elknisch-*ach*, forgive me-Herr Milhoan? These pieces are cunningly crafted and terribly difficult to restore."

"Indeed, they are, Frau Schuller. I confess it would be my first Elknisch. But I am skilled. More importantly, I am patient. As patient as he is said to have been.

"The piece, it seems, has been in your shop for some time. Might you trust me to bring it to life again? To carry the tradition, at its most skillful, at its technically strongest, to another generation of the Master?"

Their exchange of glances was *ganz in Ordnung*—entirely ordered. Each of them at the clock, at Milhoan, at one another, out the window at the bustling swirl behind him, at one another again.

Then at him. They took one another's hands without looking.

"We will talk," Frau Schuller said. "Please go and have some lunch. A liter of beer. Take a nice walk. Consider if you are capable enough for this work. Then come back."

"I think that is very gracious advice, Frau Schuller. You accord me nearly as much respect as you have for this wonderful clock."

She tried not to crinkle her eyes.

"For an American, he is quite perceptive, don't you think, my dear?" Herr Schuller stood close to her as they watched him stroll down the street toward the park.

Leo Milhoan, listening now to the wind roll across Wisconsin Avenue, around his Bridgehouse, and swirl southward down his River, laid the package on a cotton pad, with a slipcover of silk. He looked at all six sides before beginning to unwrap the soft, but thick material swaddling the clock. Frau Schuller could have transported a baby's sigh to Mars without so much as a nick if she had chosen to.

He began to make notes in his Kraftbuch, his technical notebook, for each side, each fold of packaging, beginning with the outermost cloth. Then he began gently lifting each coat of swaddling, always returning the orientation of the clock face up and top away.

When he got to the last layer, a soft parchment paper, likely conserved from a ream from the last century, he paused to still his hands.

"I think I need a breather first. Pay homage to my River. Then, I'll wash my hands again. And find a way to get inside it in order to begin figuring out how to fix it."

He wandered down the two circular cement flights to the pitwalk level.

Chapter 6:

Off the Books

Leo Milhoan reached for his cigarettes. Found an empty pocket.

"Quit them just in time to die from something else," he grumbled.

He was restless. His River was dark, cooling off from its summer excesses. Early autumn leaves dusted the pitwalk, scrunching and shusshing under his safety boots. The whole city was quiet. The moon too new to glow.

His flask was out and easily opened with one hand. He took a hard pull.

"Easy, dumbass. You've got a clock to doctor. Even nimble fingers can't dance with a numb mind." He turned his shoulder a bit to the right to tuck the Scotch away in a hip pocket.

She stared at him, gently bobbing in the water. Ten feet away. Bold. Fearless. Sizing him up.

Too shaken to speak, he stared back.

She spoke. "Hiwholthin," and touched her face with one hand. He saw her webbed fingers.

It's eaten into my brain already, he thought. Damn! That was fast.

She moved closer, smoothly. Spoke more sharply. "Hiwholthin." Touched her face again.

Insistently, "Hiwholthin!" He played it in his mind. Spoke it, "Hiwholthin." She stared at his hand.

He paused. "Leo." Touched his face.

Her eyes widened. She flung water at him with both hands, drenching his shirt and pants.

"Elinleo."

Then, she was gone, barely a swirl in the place where she dove. A faint musky aroma.

swirling into his face.

"If I weren't soaked to my underwear, I'd check myself in for a 3-day psych review. What on God's earth did I just see? Again! That's what—or who—I saw last week!"

He stood on the pitwalk for an hour. For no reason he could fathom, he looked at the River and spoke.

"Elinleo," he said boldly. Then once more, soft and shy. "Elinleo."

She had doubled back upriver, pushing hard until she was behind him, surfacing to watch him unseen as he stood looking for her, and floating silently toward him as he faced the wrong direction. Seeing his face open as the water hit him struck her as funny. She giggled, a purring sound. She silently sat on a pier behind and to the right of him, where she could watch, unobserved.

Good hands, she thought. But sick. Dying.

Amelthr-amomn. Interesting. Appealing.

Arousing.

She slipped under the darkened water and watched him carefully as he opened the interior pitwalk door to go inside. She watched his strong legs intently as he climbed the stairs. The warm light of the pit-level electrical room washed over her, silhouetting his shoulders. then snapped into darkness as the door closed behind him.

He is strong and warm, she thought.

A good one to mate.

Chapter 7:

Going Cuckoo

Laying on the work surface of his Bridgehouse, the Elknisch clock shyly yielded its secrets to Milhoan's gentle probing. He noticed a small hole on the backside along the roofline.

"Is that a wormhole? Seems a shame." He spoke in whispers when he worked this craft. "Hope the insides aren't entirely eaten away. Let's see if it runs all the way through," he soughed.

Taking a thin, stainless-steel probe from his kit, he gently passed it into the wormhole. He felt resistance, a detente.

"Hell of a hard-headed worm in there," he breathed. With a touch more pressure, a small click, and the roof smoothly opened along a hidden lateral hinge, soundlessly.

"Great-grandfather, you wily Kraut, you. What kind of latch did you invent here?"

He took several photos, made detailed sketches in his Kraftbuch, and marveled at the design and execution of the mechanism.

"It's as if you carved this latch from a brass block. Did you build a micro lathe more than a century ago, Grandfather?

"Your work is exquisite. I can't wait to show this to Ed."

Inside the clock housing, Milhoan found glorious, all but intact workmanship. Delicate gears on the backside of the face were connected to a subtly elegant, spiraling rod that ran to the clockwork drives, which in turn danced with the comparatively burly mechanics of the drive weights. Pressed between them, a side gear system popped open the sturdy cuckoo door, drove the cuckoo on her perch outwardly, moved the tiny bellows that made her sing, and then withdrew the whole show to bring the clock back to ticking repose.

He pushed back from the machinery to look with tenderness at the entire piece, a village of three different apparatuses—timekeeper, stagecraft, and performer.

"I wish I had known you." His voice barely stirred the Bridgehouse air. Milhoan lifted the clock onto his foot-high work platform as if it were a sleeping puppy.

"Let's hear you sing."

A century silent, he set the time for 11:59, then triggered the latch.

Twelve times. "Cuckoo."

The tone was beautiful. Clear. A bit of a trill at the end of each 'coo.'

"How for the love of music did you manage a trill, Herr Grossvater? There must be an extra reed. Or a bit of a brass rattle in there somewhere? No one has heard a tremolo cuckoo this century.

"My heavens! Encore!"

His agile hands smoothed across the whistles' ports on the sides, beautifully disguised as Tyrolean rafter windows.

Thirty feet away, on the edge of the pier, she heard the first sound.

Froze.

Where? What food is this?

A second later. Cuckoo. Then, again.

She thrust herself into the water, as silently as the moonlight on its surface. Looked up at the Bridgehouse window.

A third time.

It is Elinleo, she purred. Elinleo is singing. To me.

She stopped flowing toward the strange sound of unknown food. Her emotions flowed instead, following a current of fascination within her, and turning her toward him. She held still as the river currents caressed her. As Elinleo might do.

He made the call again. Again, again. She stirred powerfully.

She murmured, "*Shesmen'athuma.*"

She would mate him. With love.

Chapter 8:

Wha'hemoste Athuma
I Will Kill For Love

"Well, well. What in our Lord Jesus' name kind of thing is this to walk in on?"

Milhoan snapped from blankness toward groggy. "Must've dozed off," he mumbled.

Lester Chepstone was forty minutes early for his day shift. Typically. Any kind of torture, any opportunity to dominate, to denigrate, to flex his withered, panicked ego.

He had slipped into the Bridgehouse without the customary courtesy of first hitting the security doorbell. The Standard Operating Procedure of the underconfident, it was a rude and aggressive gesture, meant to provoke a bad response. His way of begging for the weapon of false victimhood.

"Smells like the drunk tank at the county lock-up," Chepstone mocked. "I see you've been playing with your dollhouse while you drank your Devil's brew all night long. I don't know why I even bother praying for you."

"You'll learn plenty about the county jail in person, Gonzo," Milhoan said. The nickname was hated, a cutting reminder that Milhoan knew enough about him to jack this bum directly into unemployment, after a real stay in the real county lock-up. Running a private business on City time got you fired. Running a credit card scam disguised as a ministry got you fired, plus an orange jumpsuit, and daily body cavity searches for five to seven years.

"You wretched, heathen drunk. Clean up this hell and go home before I report you." Chepstone clenched his fists. He squared off, lips shuddering with rage and fear, hoping for an excuse to take Milhoan down.

"Gonzo, my shift is over in exactly thirty-three minutes. I do not answer to you now nor to jackasses ever. You are a weak and tiny man. A bully. Get out of my Bridgehouse now and don't come back for thirty-two minutes. Do it now."

Chepstone glared at him, equal parts sanctimonious and fearful. "You'll pay, you damnable drunk," he hissed. "You'll pay in God's hell."

He fled down the stairs and slammed the security door behind him.

Milhoan listened to him stomp up the corrugated metal stairs, his expensive, leather-soled shoes slipping on the steel grates, then fast trot down the sidewalk.

"I've been in hell for years, little clown," Milhoan said. "And wear your goddam safety boots at work, you prissy dunce."

My flask. Dammit! Left it by the hand sink after I rinsed it out. He took a deep cleansing breath. "Every day, in every way, I'm getting better and better. If you count dying as better," he laughed coarsely.

The flask was gone.

"Well, hell. No sense worrying about it now. Maybe I left it on the pitwalk. A place Gonzo never goes. That's where work is done."

Milhoan swaddled the precious clock and tucked it securely into his pack. After gathering up his tools and personal belongings, he gave everything a quick wipe down with disinfectant, per work-rule protocols.

He walked carefully down the circular stairs.

Without warning, Chepstone snapped the security door open and tossed the empty flask at him. Milhoan one-handed it and tucked it into his hip pocket.

"I already sent the pictures of this, sitting by the sink, on City property no less, to Cora's email, demon drunkard! Just a little favor for you. Let the boss get a look at what I found my first morning back from vacation. Looks like I'll be working some overtime during your suspension."

Milhoan inhaled smoothly. Let his breath slip away gently. Cora Kowalski was the Bridge Operations Manager. She was also no fan of Chepstone.

"It's not that you're a consummate asshole that aggravates me, Gonzo. It's your narcissistic, 7th-grade whining. Your aching, silly scramble to climb onto others to make yourself feel taller, bigger, and better. You're fundamentally jealous. Dishonest. Most of all, you're weak. A punk puffing himself up.

"You'll never be the man your mother was."

Milhoan pushed past the paper tiger, blinking into the dawn. The clock was tucked safely and securely on his back. Flask discretely stowed on his person. A little shaky on the stairs heading topside.

"I shouldn't let that turd get under my skin," he thought. "Head home, get some real rest. I'll work on the Elknisch this afternoon when Ed gets home from school. I think I'll leave 'er home as long as that goddam boat anchor is on the whine."

She floated in a shadow, upright, grooming her coat, watching and listening to everything. She was concealed behind an old-wood pier piling that smelled like fish. And her Elinleo.

He smelled like *Shesmen'athuma*. Mate-love.

Now her eyes were hard. The harsh barking from the Other piqued sudden, cold anger. That one, that Other was *khakha'thontha*. Danger-later.

She would wait for it to slip. To look away. Stumble. Then pull it under. Not food. Just kill it. End the danger. Kill the danger.

"*Gilpanlostha*." She whispered toward Chepstone. Soon-to-be-dead.

She inhaled a deep breath, let the top of it slip out gently, and dove for hunting.

"*Wha'hemoste athuma*," she promised as she kicked toward the edge of the riverwalk where the rock bass liked to hide.

"I will kill for love."

Milhoan paused at the edge of the bridge span, gazing intuitively and intently toward the pier where she had just wafted. He glanced at the surface of the water, near where she had dived, lingering a few wistful seconds, then headed to the bus stop.

She saw him. He knew she was there.

They wanted one another. *Foumou.* Must-to-be. They would have one another. They were *wha'hemoste athuma.* They would kill for love.

She growled as she grabbed a fat walleye. *Foumou shesmen'athuma* first. She was hungry for more than food.

Later *gilpanlostha.* Good *gilpanlostha.*

Chapter 9

Shesmen'athuma
Mate-Love

There is a time between nightfall and daybreak when there is no time at all.

There manifests instead a rift, a border without flaw, a not quite coming together of this and of that, where things neither blend into the other nor stand quite separately on their own.

The Bridgehouse was still, holding its breath until the sun began to pre-dawn color itself into the last of the night.

Milhoan put down his tools. The clock was nearly restored.

"I'll leave the finishing for the boy to do with me," he said softly. "Then he'll know the clock is his."

He and Ed had worked diligently on it together over the past week. Or was it longer than that? Milhoan was having difficulty keeping track of the days. His life only cohered in the Now.

He had resolved the debate between rushing to finish it as a gift before death showed up or to save the incomplete work, so they might finish it together before death took him.

"No time like the rapidly failing present," he said to his River. "I'll give that precious bonehead my tools tomorrow with the clock. We'll have time, I hope, to do just enough work so that I'm sure he can finish it properly. That way, he'll know what to do with the tools after I'm gone.

"The precious artifacts of experience are in this kit as well. Might give him the hip flask as well.

"I sure love that boy."

He watched the moon move for an hour.

"Yeah. I think I'll add something interesting to our legacy. Sneak in a secret. A gift from my grave to support our legacy. Something that carries us on together in some way. I think I know what to do. He's a bright boy. I think he can handle it well.

"If I had just one more goddam year."

The sting of tears bit him hard.

He shook himself. "To hell with that. To hell with you Leo for dying. To hell with you, Rob, for trying. To hell with everything."

He looked through the Bridgehouse window at his River.

Despair exhausted itself by its presence. He took a deep breath. Wiped his eyes. Blew his nose.

"Ok, buddy. That'll do. No more of that. If these are your last months or days, then there's no time left for ranting, regrets, or ridicule. There is, however, time for a wee nip, thank the gods for that! I have fewer of them to enjoy, day by day."

His mind gradually fell into stillness, calming further as his work boots landed on each stair like rocks falling onto wet sand. He brushed against the spiral sidewall to keep steadily downward to his River.

The pitwalk door leaned nearly as hard into him as he into it.

"Tired tonight," he thought.

Once on the pitwalk, safety lights out, crescent moon abandoning all the urban edges in favor of the flow of organic ambivalence, he tipped his flask. The River moved with insouciance, seeking a bottom, fleeing artifice and artificial light, defiant in Her incompressible blood, and yielding only to the touch at the edges of Her endless flow.

The River became aware of Milhoan but restrained calling to him. Soon enough, River thought. Soon enough.

When Hiwholthin suddenly crested the surface in front of him, Milhoan barely stirred.

"Hello, sweet being. Wonderful Hiwholthin," he said softly. "How beautiful you are."

"Elinleo," she purred. A moment later she pushed under the safety railing and pulled herself fluidly onto the pitwalk.

She was nearly as tall as he, lithe and liquid arms and legs, mouth set. Eyes nearly glowing. Her fur was dark brown with water, nearly as smooth as skin, as fine as a precious weave.

"Elinleo," she said again and touched his face. She pulled at his shirt. "Are you serious?"

He knew the answer. She pulled again, harder, leaning against him urgently. He tried to work at his first button, as she watched impatiently. He got the top one loose. She gripped the bottom one, fumbled it, and pulled the next three off. A moment later the shirt lay in a pile on the concrete pitwalk.

She stared at his chest. Touched his hair there, then her own, caressing both of them. It seemed to take forever before he stood naked, but a mere second for her to leap onto him, wrapping her legs around his waist, then pushing him inside her. He thrust forward but she stopped him, pulling him instead against the safety railing.

She would be in charge of this, it was clear. It was the way.

A moment later, they were both in the water, under the surface. He struggled to free himself. She held him under until he became still. Then she crested them both to the surface, still wrapped around him.

"Elinleo," she whispered to him. He gulped air greedily. She waited for him to calm.

"*Shesmen'athuma,*" she said and pulled him deeper inside her. They gasped together at the bracing urgency of her tugging. Her legs tightened around him. They floated together.

"I don't know what you're saying, Hiwholthin. We are in our River. It seems I am firmly in your hands. Among other things. Now what?"

"*Shesmen'athuma,*" she said again, urgently, imploring, expecting of him an answer to a question he did not understand.

Her eyes gleamed brighter. She took his shoulders and shifted, just once, closer to him.

"*Shesmen'athuma,*" she said, her voice demanding now, willing him to respond to her.

He stared into her eyes and scanned her brown face, surprised to realize that he had never loved before like this, knowing that he loved her as much as his own kin and kind. That he loved her as he had never, and would never again.

"Hiwholthin." His voice shook. He felt a familiar virility, one that had abandoned him long ago.

She felt him swell inside her. Urgently, she whispered "*Shesmen'athuma*" and ground her heels into his back.

"*Shesmen'athuma*," he said suddenly. "My heavens, of course! You have invited me. Accept the invitation, Leo, you old dunce! We can't love without inviting it. Can't mate without mutual consent, the shared yes before we share ourselves.

"Yes, Hiwholthin! Yes, I consent. I accept you. *Shesmen'athuma*, precious Hiwholthin."

She instantly began to vibrate her inner walls, throbbing her mate lust against and around him. They were locked together, without either penetration or withdrawal. Her trembling moved from their bond, through their thighs, arms, breasts, and bellies. The autumn water was cool. He couldn't tell if he was vibrating with her or shivering from the cold.

She felt the difference. Immediately began to slowly spin them in the River, first one way then the other. The slow twirl somehow warmed them both. And intensified their touch at the same time.

"*Shesmen'athuma*." They said it together. Her eyes blazed, webbed fingers caressing his back, his buttocks, probing him, entering him.

She locked eyes with him again. He understood.

"*Shesmen'athuma*." Together. They sent rapid ripples across their River.

Shesmen'athuma. Each time, they vibrated together more intensely. He pulled her against him and gently bit her neck. She gasped, leaned back far enough to bite his lip, just shy of pain. She quivered harder, focusing every sparkle of her energy into their connection.

Suddenly she leaned away from him, pulling him deeper inside, tore his hands from her backside, and pushed them against her breasts. She bent back further until her head was underwater. She locked onto him so hard that he could not move, could not ejaculate, could not wilt.

Pulling him into her deeper. Deeper still. Locking him into place.

She threw his hands off her breasts and forced them to her buttocks, pushed his finger inside her, forcing herself onto him, pulling him hard onto her.

Without warning, she pushed him backward, now his face underwater. His instincts forced him to struggle.

"*Shesmen'athuma*," she called from the air.

He said it underwater, submitting to his imminent death by drowning.

She instantly pulled him up to her face caressing his with the backs of her hands.

He began to weep tenderly. Happily. Gratefully. She was water to his fire, air to his earth.

"*Shesmen'athuma. Shesmen'athuma. Shesmen'athuma.* Hiwholthin."

He watched her tears flow. Without warning, she became gentle, caressing his back, pressing her lips to his heart, reaching out to hold his hands, tenderly touching his palms with soft fingertips, purring harshly.

Then she was still. Her eyes blazed and she leaned forward until their noses touched.

"Elinleo," she whispered and waited.

"Hiwholthin," he whispered back. "Always and for good, Hiwholthin. *Shesmen'athuma.*"

She released the pressure on his penetration, immediately wave after wave of climax pounded inside her before he could prepare for it. Again and again, he poured himself into her. She stared into his eyes and moved back and forth, hands on his back to pull him deeper, then to push him out. Time after time after time, until he lost track of time.

As he faded out of consciousness, he whispered, "*Shesmen'athuma. Hiwholthin.*"

From another time and space, he felt her press her lips to his ear. "*Shesmen'athuma,* Elinleo."

Dawn crept up onto his waking. He was still naked, in the Bridgehouse, laying in a nest of his own damp clothing, a small weave of wet birchbark tied gently to his manhood.

"Hiwholthin!" he called out. Groggy, confused, urgently.

She peered at him from the top of the stairs, purring.

"Elinleo," she said tenderly, touched him intimately, touched her nose to his, and waited for him to settle and focus on her eyes. Then she slipped silently down the stairs. He heard her splash—intentionally—at him a moment later.

"I love you," he said.

He scrambled to his feet.

"I love you," he called out the window, to her, to the world. To Death itself.

When he looked down to the River, she was gone.

"*Sheshmen'athuma,* Hiwholthin."

Elinleo, she mouthed underwater. *Shesmen'athuma.*

She turned toward her *thiflessla.* Once inside, she fluffed her nest of reeds and prairie grasses harvested from their River's edges.

She lay down and stretched. There was a new searing deep inside her, next to her First.

She was Second. She was *thipthipetha.* Fulfilled. Finally. She would fulfill her duty, her lineage.

Thynda'undan. She would swim ahead.

Tomorrow she would return to her Elinleo. Tomorrow. For more.

Chapter 10:

Lucid Visions

"Leo!

"I had a last-minute cancellation. Told the staff to beat feet for home as soon as you got here. So glad you called at the luckiest possible time."

Dr. Rob Schafhirt rushed around his desk to shake hands. They clapped each other on the back, awkwardly and with real affection.

"Oh, shit, Leo. Is that too much?"

"Still a pretty damn tough dude, Rob. Not one of the dainty types. Only real trouble I have is between my ears. Like that my whole life. If you could knock that out of me, you'd have done it by now, and be suing me over the bill."

"Damn right. On both counts. Probably ruin both a good tungsten surgical hammer and a crappy litigation attorney along the way."

"Hey, I'm standing right here, for hell's sake. Mumble that crazy shit to the door after I leave, will ya?"

"Shut up and park your ass. Care for a wee dram?"

"Like rice cares for white, I would."

They toasted one another.

"Thanks for not toasting my health, Rob."

"Christ, if it were that easy, I'd have done that for you, then the whole world, and then retired to bored fishing and zithering years ago."

They swirled Scotch in their glasses, warming it with their hands through the glass, popping their noses past the rim to get a full experience.

"Not bad, Rob. Not bad at all," Leo said.

"Damn straight."

They sipped, looking at straggling golden leaves clinging to barren twigs. The office was comfortably austere. Rob's desk on one side, but a real living room feel on the other. They both felt at home in the space. Easy chairs, side by side, facing a spacious window.

"OK, Leo. What's going on?"

They stared, side by side, at ease and watching nothing at all through the window for a few minutes.

"It's beginning to make me crazy, Rob."

Schafhirt stifled his gasp. "I understand, Leo. I worried it might progress fast. Science has little help to offer to moderate these experiences. Especially with a stubborn hellion like you, who won't just lay down and die. I wish you were less admirable—I'd just write a note to your boss declaring you medically incompetent for the work. But I know that's what gives you meaning as a man. A toasted marshmallow. That you are.

"Let's get you a consult with a death doula. Dying isn't for the weak of heart."

"Bullshit, Rob. You're missing my point. Death isn't making me crazy. That old Greek bastard Socrates said 'death is the cure for life.' He was right.

It's the goddam disease making me crazy, not a fear of death. I am seeing things, Rob. Wild, intense, and as real as can be things. Not just seeing, but hearing, feeling. Experiencing. They seem so real. They shouldn't be real, but I feel them that way.

"These hallucinations—if that's even the right word—are also making me happy. I am happier than I have been most of my life. Is it a symptom of disease if it makes you happy? Can't dying admit of joy, too?"

They looked through the window at the dead grass where brown, red, and gold leaves were settling in for the winter.

"Lemme just get this straight," Rob said. "You scheduled an urgent appointment with me with a Chief Complaint of 'being happy'? You understand insurance is not going to cover this."

"Insurance can bugger off," Leo smiled.

"I'll drink to that." Rob poured again. "Let's be serious while I doctor you. Are you sure these are hallucinations? Are they provoking any thoughts of harming yourself? Or others?"

"No, no, and no. OK, I guess we could call them hallucinations, but those are just things you see, right? I'm experiencing smells, tastes, and skin feelings. You can't hallucinate an orgasm, can you, Rob?"

"That would be a ticket to riches beyond anyone's dreams, my friend." He paused with impish intent. "But if it's possible, can I freeze your carcass and try to make some cash with this? I've got kids going to college soon."

"Won't matter to me what you do. I won't live there anymore."

They laughed hard together.

"Is love just a hallucination, Rob? And if it is, does it really matter to an everyday geezer like me? Isn't love enough?"

"My dear friend, love is always enough. And so are you."

Rob shifted his chair to peer straight on at Leo. "No bullshitting now. Tell me more about these visions. Your safety is the issue here, not that your mind is firing on unexpected cylinders."

"You just want the dirty parts?"

"Leo, I don't personally, but I'm still your goddam doctor and I want to understand what's going on. I need to be sure you're safe."

Leo sighed. "I hear you, Rob. Sometimes I can be a little too much."

"Cheers to that," Rob said, smiling. He poured generously.

"Not like hallucinations. More intense. More real. We dropped acid in the 70s. We know what that is. These experiences are nothing like that shitty, chemical excuse for an adventure. These are indistinguishable from the rest of my reality. Except that the content, the stuff that's actually going on, is beyond my ken."

They sipped. Falling leaves rotated in the evening sun.

"Tell me anything that you feel comfortable sharing, Leo. I'm going to sit and listen."

Leo sighed, happily.

"As I said, these are more intense than a hallucination. More real than reality. More like a parallel or an alternative experience, completely in synch with my normal life except for the stuff that's going on. I'm not afraid of them, ever.

"I've been having this love affair, Rob. Hell, it's crazier to say it out loud than to experience it."

"That's as good a description of a love affair as I've ever heard, buddy."

Leo leaned across the gap between their chairs and held Rob's arm firmly.

"I am having a love affair, a sexual love affair, with some kind of human-like water creature. Not human, not animal. Fully intelligent. Kind. Strong. She's pregnant—relax, asshole, not by me. She lives in the River somewhere close to my Bridgehouse.

"I haven't ever loved like this, Rob. Ever."

The sun coasted slowly toward the moon, tapping a golden leaf free here and there along its arc. Venus began to glow.

"It's a pretty rich hallucination that allows you to know that she's pregnant, Leo."

"I agree. If I was making it all up, I sure as hell wouldn't build that into the fantasy. She has shown me her belly. I'm an old man, but I know what a preggers belly looks like, for hell's sake."

Rob touched his arm gently. "Remember, friend, I'm not challenging the reality of your experience. I'm a doctor, a bio-scientist, remember. I am damn curious about everything. Moreso because I care about you.

"Leo, these sorts of mermaid stories are integral to human mythology across time and culture. The disease may be triggering your deep mind to release these as felt experiences, which we pitiable moderns might categorize as hallucinations or some other psycho-emotional pathology."

Leo nodded. "But she is not a mermaid. Those are half-human. She is a hominid, more human than animal, but a singular, distinct kind of being. Not an amalgamation. A real being. That's what matters."

"Sounds like you're having quite a time of it?"

"It's so real, Rob. She has her own language. Where the hell would I get that from if not from her? She wants me, goddammit. Wants to be with me, to be my lover. To love me. She has desires for me. She loves me.

"And I love her. Wildly. Like no one ever.

"It sounds crazy to say, but it all feels perfectly normal: we are in love with each other. She must know that I'm dying. She, well, she sniffs my ears and mouth and nose. And then she's quiet, touches me gently, caring about me. She cares about me, Rob. And I do care for her as well.

"She comes to the Bridgehouse every night I'm there. Sometimes she takes me into the water. She knows I'm no match for her swimming. She's strong, man. Very strong. And she keeps me warm in the water—it's getting colder by the day—just by holding me."

Leo paused to empty his glass.

"She keeps me warm by making love with me."

"In the water?" Rob sipped and looked through the window. Avoided eye contact.

"Yes."

Crows gathered in the nearly barren tree outside the office window, looking for opportunities.

"Are you afraid of her?"

"I am exhilarated by her, Rob, but never afraid of her. At least no more afraid than I am of love itself. Thank you for asking that question."

The streetlights came on, aggravating the irritable crows to flight. A bus went by, stirring up silent leaves in its wake. Rob poured again.

"Basically, she's screwing your brains out?" Rob looked assiduously out the window, holding his breath for the answer.

Leo fixed the side of his head with a hard gaze.

"That's pretty funny, really. I'll laugh later. Yes. She is. But no. Not at all, Rob. *That* hallucination I could deal with. Erotic mentation thanks to the literally sick shit in my brain? Not a bad way to die.

"But this isn't that. We *love*, Rob. We love each other. My God, I care about her. I'm not that far gone. Or am I?"

Rob reached to turn the salt lamp beside him on, adjusting the glow to something suitable.

"Leo, I'm still your doctor. Far, far more importantly, I am always your friend. So, I am going to ask you one and only one more question."

"How am I going to pay your fee?"

"Clearly the disease has not infected your wise ass. Goddammit, Leo, this is important."

Leo poured; it was his turn. They sipped. Night opened into the room.

Rob spoke softly. "Is there any chance that she's putting you at risk? Any violence whatsoever? Any chance of any high-risk behavior of any kind? Anything at all that could harm you?"

Leo sipped, watching a leaf circle past the window.

"What I'm getting at, Leo, is this: is there any chance that this is a run-up to suicide? I have to tell you, the making love in the water part definitely worries me. Are you sure—and I will believe you if you'll tell me that you are not—are you sure that you haven't any suicidal ideation? More to your reality, that she is strong enough to rescue you if you should lose consciousness in the water?"

"Suicide is always a no-go for me, Rob. Even a shitty life is precious. You know that I've been suicidal exactly once in my life."

"When Evy died. I remember that very well, Leo. She was a remarkable woman."

"Yes, she was. I never bothered to fall in love after her. You and I worked through that together. I will be on this Earth or in Hiwholthin's water until my natural death."

"That is her name?"

"Yes. It is more beautiful when she says it.

"As for her strength, it is impressive. She hasn't, but I'm pretty sure she could pick me up, could move me through the river without much exertion, and lift me to safety.

"Rob, I love her. She loves me. I wish I could have the rest of my life with her."

A crescent moon beamed over the trees in complete silence.

"Ha. Come to think of it, I guess I do have the rest of my life with her."

Rob went to his desk. Sent an email home.

"Leo, let me put your mind at ease. First, I agree that it is medically possible this is a side effect of the disease working on your brain. hence into your mind. But so damn what? If you're in love with an otter-like hominid, whether for real or as a hallucination, what difference does it really make?

"None, Leo. That's the answer. It makes no difference at all.

"You are in love. That's it. That's all that matters. My God, man. ninety percent of humankind is not in love at this very moment. No, my friend. There is nothing, nothing wrong with this. There is nothing wrong with love."

The room fell silent, save the movement of their breath.

"Are you happy to be with her, Leo? Are you happy for you?"

Leo lifted his glass, touched his mouth to it as if he were kissing her.

"Like I've never been my entire life. She inspired me to finish the Edenkoben clock with Ed. I've already given the kid my tools and clock workers contact list. Everything. He'll carry that legacy forward.

"I'm confident that she loves me, too. I've been helpful to women. I've been handy for women. But honestly, I've never been loved by a woman. Not even by Evy.

"Hiwholthin loves me."

Rob sipped. Closed his eyes and took a moment to enjoy the quiet.

"Leo, the only thing better than living well is dying well. I am entirely happy for you. And for her.

"Let's have another wee dram and think about love until all the stars are out. Then I'll see to us getting safe rides home."

"Best goddam prescription you've ever written, Rob. Thank you."

Chapter 11:

Crazy In Love

Leo clawed toward waking up, alert but confused.

I am laying down, he thought. Staring at a ceiling, familiar but strange. My left side is cool but my right side is warm. Why is that? Is this how a fatal brain disease progresses? Strange as hell. Or heaven.

He was more curious than afraid. Impatient with limitation, not yet resigned to death. He took a deep breath, nose tingling with a mossy, warm, comfortable, and safe aroma.

"Hiwholthin," he whispered. She always lay at his right side.

She stirred against him, her strong leg resting across his thighs, claiming his manhood for herself. He pushed gently against her soft, rich fur, her strength.

One arm cradling his neck, she smoothed her right hand across his belly and chest, curling up to touch his cheek. She began to purr in her way, sharing her contentment without hesitation or restraint.

"Elinleo," her voice birred wetly, pressing her breasts into his side. She touched the tip of her tongue to his cheek.

He squirmed his neck to turn just far enough to see the sky through the Bridgehouse window, without moving anything else. False dawn, he thought. We've at least one precious hour more like this, just like this. If only we had years.

My gods, I am happy. I am actually happy. Truly happy. Everything about this feels unreal, even insane, but I am not crazy. It is real. My mind is clear enough to know love.

I am in love with Hiwholthin.

A tear, just one, but massive, slid from the corner of his eye, rolling backward across his face toward his ear.

Her cheek blocked it and she stirred enough to kiss it from his skin, purring. She wriggled closer still to him, so strong that she pushed him across the blanket he had lain on the concrete floor for them to share.

The heat from her belly poured into his waist, pressing into him, all but healing him with fire. She is with child, he thought. This I know for certain.

Will I live long enough to see her give birth? I don't know how to help her, but her mate is...where? Except me. I am her mate now. But what would she even need from me?

He turned thought after thought over in his mind, fretting about her and the child, worrying for them, afraid he might not be good enough to provide for them, even in the short time he had left.

A twinge of jealousy toward her mate. He'll never see his own child, he thought. May I live long enough, with wits enough, to hold her wee one.

I will love her baby, too.

He pulled her closer to him, pressing his arm against the back of her shoulders, turning just enough to rest a hand on her waist, close to her child.

Maybe all this is just a dream, just the disease causing me an elaborate hallucination. It's nutty to believe any of this is even possible, much less real. But I know love when I feel it. No matter how long it's been.

I know love.

He sighed, just once, inhaling her scent as deeply as he could.

Can you hallucinate an aroma? He slowly turned his head back to her, eyes closed, and kissed her brow. Her redolence stirred him as he licked the taste of her from his lips. Well, an erotic hallucination is better than brooding over plans for a real funeral. I'll count that as optimism.

She felt him shift, purred again, pressed her mouth to his ear, bit him gently. Fully awake now. Feeling the impertinent, impending dawn.

"*Shesmen'athuma*, Elinleo."

Her whisper was insistent, pleading. Fierce.

"Yes, sweet Hiwholthin. *Shesmen'athuma.*"

His voice was as soft as the indigo sky. He felt himself swelling, surprised that he could still respond to her urgency.

She was on top of him in a breath, straddling him, pressing herself against his belly and thighs, pushing onto his hardness, locking him inside her. She pushed his shoulders against the floor hard, but comfortably.

He cupped her hips and pretended to struggle. She throbbed inside instantly, eyes glowing at him with devotion.

"*Shesmen'athuma.*" They invited each other, sharing their hoarse whispers, holding each other timelessly, pinned against and into the other.

"Elinleo," she purred, touching her nose to his, cupping his manhood tenderly as he ran the tips of his fingers across her waist, backside, and thighs.

"Sweet Hiwholthin."

His voice wavered as she released him inside her and they writhed until they crested together, river and shore, water and air, invigorated and exhausted by love.

Chapter 12:

Jesus Wept

Aside from the melodic hum of electrical relays two floors below and the soft glow on the ceiling cast by the red, amber, and green indicator lights from the Operator's panel beside him, Leo Milhoan's Bridgehouse was as silent and as dark as it got. As close to home as he had.

Hiwholthin's aroma was everywhere, and he happily took one deep breath of her after another until his lips tingled and the room spun.

"She definitely makes me dizzy," he chuckled. "I think we set some kind of a *shesmen'athuma* record tonight. No wonder she had to go feed. I'm ready for a sandwich myself."

Suddenly he grabbed for the control panel as weakness washed him into his chair.

"Damn, that's new. Making great progress toward dyin', Rob!" he shouted to the ceiling and slumped forward, giggling at the simple stupidity of remaining alive in the face of death.

"I used to think dying was pretty straightforward. This thing I've got is a surprise a minute." He rested his head on his arm until his fingers went numb.

"To hell with it. I'm too tired to eat right now."

He tried to fetch another blanket from his bag but found himself slipping from his chair gently to the floor instead. He was too weak to struggle back into the chair.

"Honey! I'm home," he sniggered. "At least I won't be too cold. Got my blanket. I can use my pack as a pillow. A wee snort, strictly a pre-embalming medicinal. Take a nap for a few hours. Tidy up. Blow Hiwholthin a kiss on my way home to a proper bed. And try like heaven itself not to die, if just for one more day."

He managed to set a wake-up alarm on his phone and fell softly into easy darkness.

"You can't murder a demon bastard if it is terminally ill."

The voice, more a croak, dripped with malice.

Leo snapped fully awake but lay completely still. Someone was in the Bridgehouse. Fear force cleared his mind and froze his body into perfect stillness.

I know that voice, he thought. But it's nothing but hate.

"Can't murder a freakish sinner if he commits suicide, can you, demon fornicator?"

The infernal voice betrayed madness, an execrable malevolence. It embodied the single-minded hate of the madman. He finally connected it.

Chepstone.

Heart pounding, Leo lay still. Chepstone must be crouched low to the floor, he thought, nearly all the way up the circular concrete stairwell. Out of reach, but not far. How the hell did he get in here? He's been reassigned to Sanitation. Too many complaints and altercations on Bridges. Shouting scriptures at passersby. His Bridgehouse keycard was supposed to be deactivated. What is the bastard doing here?

"You are a demon," Chepstone snarled.

"You savaged me out of my job, thou drunken servant of the Abaddon. Now, I come like a thief in the night with the wrath of our Lord and Savior. His vengeance has come to you in my form. For I am sent of God to give you your doom. I am the angel of the Lord your God. Come to cast you into hell, you heathen bastard."

"Gonzo." Leo's voice was somehow steady. "You need to leave this Bridgehouse immediately. Right now. Leave now and go home." His feigned bravery forced calm strength into the words.

A dozen confused plans filled his mind at once. Fight him. Call 911. Grab the marine radio and call for help. Let damn Gonzo talk himself out of whatever he is up to. Keep him talking long enough to think. That's it. Let him talk. Wait for a chance to escape.

"Do not speak, demon. Get thee behind me."

Chepstone moved so suddenly, Leo barely got an arm up before the rope slipped over his head, trapping his right elbow against his face, tearing the skin on his arm, and bending his neck fiercely.

"I will liberate God's breath of life from your evil body and save the world for Our Lord." Chepstone yanked the rope so hard that Leo's feet left the floor.

"No," Leo croaked. "Stop it, you crazy bastard! HELP!"

"Satan will not help you, thou dark servant of hell. God has sent me in His Holy Name. Praise Him. Even now your voice blasphemes Him."

He pulled Leo sharply back to the floor, slapping his head and neck. Dazed, Leo kicked wildly at anything and got in a lucky blow to Chepstone's knee. He fell awkwardly away from Leo, a dull sound as his head butted against the stainless-steel operator's panel.

As Chepstone fell backward, he pulled the rope tighter, collapsing the blood vessels on the left side of Leo's neck.

"Come to the water, demon, where you will meet your hell."

Chepstone ran down the stairs, yanking the rope savagely. Leo's body bashing into the wall, his hips pounding onto each stair.

"Help me!" Leo shouted. "Help!"

This is how I end, he thought. This punk bastard is going to drown me. What a way to go.

Oh, Hiwholthin! I shall miss you so!

Burning tears, searing pain in his neck and his trapped arm, and the shock of Chepstone's frenzied cruelty overran his will to fight.

Idiot Gonzo, he thought. I am dying. Why should I fight this shithead? Help me to die in my River. Yes! Do it! You will die in prison. That is justice for both of us. Except that I win. Two more steps down, out the door, and into the River. Go, asshole. Go!

Leo willed himself to go limp.

A low rumble flew toward the lower-level stairs, sharp and fast.

Hiwholthin leaped onto Chepstone's back. Grabbing his eyes with both hands, she yanked his head to the left. Then sank her teeth into his exposed neck.

Leo fell, disoriented and dazed onto the concrete floor, flat against an electrical closet. Blinded, the rope tangled in his arms, Chepstone flailed at her. He made a sound so hideous that no animal would have claimed it.

Hiwholthin viciously pushed his hands away, shook her head, and tore the muscles off the base of his skull with the first bite.

Chepstone's head lolled stupidly to the left, his ear bouncing up and down on his shoulder.

"Mommy! Oh, Mommy. Oh, Jesus. Save me!" he screamed.

Hiwholthin tore his carotid artery and throat out with the second bite. Then yanked his head back to the right so hard that Leo felt the snapping bones vibrating down the rope.

Chepstone's arms went limp. He fell across Leo, Hiwholthin's fingers still driven up to the webbings into his eyes. She dragged him by the sockets, dead, across the bloody concrete floor, through the security door she had battered down, and onto the pitwalk.

A moment later, Leo heard a heavy splash, then silence.

They were gone.

He crawled through Chepstone's gore onto the pitwalk, thrashing at the noose still looped around his neck.

"Hiwholthin!" he rasped. His voice had no power. Still, he called to her. Again and again, then he fell silent and exhausted.

False dawn shook him awake. He was covered with blood, weak. Dried blood made his arms stiff. His neck hurt like hell itself. Worse, he was at a loss to understand what happened.

Someone mugged me in the Bridgehouse, he thought. But who? And how? No one can get into a secure Bridgehouse.

"Dammit to hell," he rasped. "Who on Earth would beat me like this?" He twisted himself toward the Bridgehouse door.

My gods, he thought wildly. It was Hiwholthin? Please, no. Please!

He remembered. She had been here. Thick blood was streaked across the concrete floor just inside. On the edge of it, clearly, one of her footprints.

Hiwholthin attacked me? Why? What did I do? She has nearly killed me. I need to get back into the Bridgehouse, up to the control level, back to safety. Call for help.

He tried to stand up, but his head wouldn't follow his body. Frustrated with rage, he tried to pull himself up, but his arm was missing.

"Goddammit all into endless hell. My mind is so fried that I've managed to lose my own arm." He fell hard on his backside onto the pitwalk outside.

"Maybe I am already dead," he said, suddenly calm. "Still got the same old man's voice. So, I guess that means that hell is just more of life. Damn it all, I was afraid of that.

"Where is my goddam arm?"

He heard his watch ticking.

"Why is my watch in my ear? Sonofabitch, I hate being dead!" He brought his left wrist up to his face. Found his other hand resting on top of his head. Felt around some more and found the rope hitched across the right side of his head and neck.

"That's a rope. Jesus God! Did I try to hang myself? I'm in love like I've never been, I'm gonna die any week now, and I decided to kill myself now? What kind of crazy shit is going on?"

He rolled around on the pitwalk for several minutes before he loosened the rope enough to free his other hand. He tore the noose off his neck, never noticing that it fell twenty feet into the pit beside him.

His legs were aching, bruised, and bloodied. His pants were torn. The right boot missing.

"There's no way I did this to myself. She was here. But Hiwholthin would not, my gods, please let me believe that she would not hurt me. Would she?

"No, Leo-boy. She did not hurt me. She would not."

He managed to get up a level to the bathroom. Washed his face and hands. Made a cold compress for his neck wounds.

As Leo climbed the stairs to the bathroom, Hiwholthin moved fast downriver. She furiously dragged the dead meat behind her, still pulling it by the eye sockets. She crossed to the opposite shore and half a block downstream of the *thiflessa* before she broke to breathe.

An old woman pushing a stolen grocery cart filled with her life's possessions glanced at her.

"You better get out of that water, sweetie. You'll catch a cold," she called down from the Clybourn Bridge sidewalk.

Hiwholthin looked at her with kindness and purred at her. Then dove, dragging the meat behind her. Near Buffalo Street, she pulled the carcass upward and stuffed it under the cross members of a floating dock, enough underwater that the carp would clean it before it began to stink.

This thing would never be food. Never. *Gilpan-khakthak.* Poisoned meat.

She turned and swam hard upstream, slowing long enough to spin only once, shaking all the stench of the *gilpan-khakthak* from her hands, mouth, and fur. She had to get back to her *shesmen'athuma,* her Elinleo.

He was injured and afraid. Elinleo!

Breaking the surface, she gulped air fast and dove again, finally coming up near his bridge. She slowed. Crested. Hid in the shadows. Listening.

The *shesmen'athuma* was talking to himself.

Elinleo is alive! Talking!

A moment later she padded across the pitwalk and peeked intensely inside the lowest level of the Bridgehouse. Leo was working to clean the blood-stained floor. Yes. Blood betrayed the kill. Good Elinleo.

Suddenly, she was standing in the doorway. Leo froze. He could feel the presence. Chepstone again?

He whirled, holding the mop handle out like a pike.

She was beautiful.

"Elinleo," she cooed. Suddenly was on him, holding him close, purring into his chest. Touching his wounds. She raced back to the pitwalk, dove into their river, and rushed back with clean moss.

"Elinleo," she purred, and her eyes filled with tears as she gently packed the rope wound on his neck with the healing herb. She touched his face, rubbed her nose on his chest, held him close, breathing him in.

"Hiwholthin, I love you. You saved my life." Tears streaked his face. She touched them, licked his cheeks, tugged at his hands, and pulled him close to her.

A moment later she pulled his erection into her again, gently.

Shesmen'athuma," they whispered back and forth until, slowly, they reached their peak.

He slumped to the floor, exhausted, unable to stand anymore. She helped him to dress, purring at him all the while. Then she carefully pushed him up the stairs to his chair. Firmly sat him down. Pulled a blanket over his shoulders.

She rushed back to the lowest level, using more moss and water to scrub all the blood away. She looked fiercely at the bloody mophead and tossed it into the pit.

Then she hurried back up to the Operator's level.

"Elinleo."

She held his face tenderly and caressed his neck until the first sunbeam came through the window. She touched his cheeks again, caressed his head, then raced down the stairs. She entered the water silently but splashed up at him as he looked with aching tenderness at her from the window. Then she dove.

Chapter 13:

Love Nourishes

Leo Milhoan put his feet up on the Bridgehouse desk and relaxed. This was his space, his River home, his workshop. His life.

Chepstone was permanently gone. The cops found his body well downriver from Leo's bridge. Still fuzzy on the details of that night, he frowned.

"To hell with it," he said firmly to the bridge control panel. "That crazy bastard is dead. Died before I did. Good riddance, shithead."

In the days just after the attack, Leo hid the Chepstone wounds. As a lone worker, there was barely a notice of him from his bosses, coworkers, or cops looking for the missing former Bridge Operator.

There wasn't any evidence left in his Bridgehouse. None that he knew of at least.

Hiwholthin cleaned it all away.

"That's one benefit to being old, sick, and dying," he said aloud. "No one wants to look at you anyway. Except for sweet Hiwholthin. She's been visiting me every single evening this week. My God, Abe, I shall miss her."

The tall man in the long coat nodded and smiled.

"You don't have much of a reputation for smiling, Abe. Weight of war, I reckon."

The tall man nodded again, sagely. He looked through the Bridgehouse window, too. Fall was well-advanced. The sun settled into darkness earlier each evening. Now, just a little past 5, little more than a glow in the west.

"War and that bullet you took. Helluva speech you made here, just down the street. Wish we had listened to you better."

Abe turned from the window and sat down in the chair next to Leo, smiling gently. He crossed his long legs with ease, leaning ever so slightly toward his host.

"I reckon you've shown up to tell me something, but you haven't said a word since you got here. I always wondered what your voice sounded like. I read once that you're a little high-pitched. Seems odd for a tall guy like you."

Abe tipped his head back a little and laughed heartily. Silently. He smiled even more broadly.

"Just between you and me, Abe, you've been dead for damn near 160 years. I'm guessing you showed up tonight to ease me over to your side of the fence," Leo said. "I told Rob two days ago I figured I was closing in on it. I feel good, you know. Mostly. But things just keep getting wackier and wackier. Just like Rob said they would.

"Of course, I may as well work. I ain't the first nor the last crazy shit in a Bridgehouse, Abe, that's for sure. Plus, there ain't any boats running this late in the season. Inspections and maintenance only, and I'm ignoring both of them.

"I'd rather kick off at work where I can pretend to be useful than in a chair at home where the family will have to futz around trying to get my carcass out the back door."

Abe nodded in agreement. Reached out and all but grasped Leo's arm with kindness.

"Plus, I couldn't see Hiwholthin if I were home. I shoulda bought that damn houseboat when I had the chance. You think she'll show up tonight?"

Abe nodded confidently, his smile broad and encouraging.

"Well, I couldn't have asked for two better traveling companions than a great President and the most wonderful, loving being I might have ever hoped to know."

Abe pointed a thumb at his own chest and raised his eyebrows.

Leo laughed hard. "Now, c'mon, Abe. You're generous as hell to help me over the fence, but we ain't gonna be lovers."

Abe gently turned his head toward the Bridgehouse stairs.

"I heard her, too, Mr. President. She's a rascal. Silent as snow when she wants to be and noisy as hell when she needs your attention."

Abe gestured kindly toward the stairs. Hiwholthin stood near the top, looking at both men, quizzically at Abe, then lovingly at Leo.

She took the last steps like water flowing upstream.

"Elinleo," she said, beaming at Leo.

"Hiwholthin, my sweet love. I'm afraid Abe being here is proof that I'll leave you soon. I hope I'll find a way to find you again. If there's any damn justice in this universe, I will find you. I'll spend all my afterlife trying to get back to you, dearest love. I promise. I promise."

She took his hand and rubbed her nose on his, purring softly.

"Elinleo."

Abraham Lincoln stood, tipped his hat at Hiwholthin, and melted through the Bridgehouse wall with the last of the sunshine.

She watched him go. Then took both of Leo's hands.

"*Shesmen'athuma*, Elinleo," she said, as softly as rain on their River.

"*Shesmen'athuma*, Hiwholthin," he whispered. "Though I don't know if I'll be able to do much for you. I seem to be getting weak faster and faster."

They gazed a long time into each other's eyes, awash in love and tears.

She helped him to his feet and guided him down the spiral stairs to the pit level. The air was cool and crisp in the twilight. She gently undressed him, kissing him all over, touching him as softly as moonlight, until he was naked and just beginning to shiver.

Hiwholthin picked him up and dove into the water.

"I'm surprised, Hiwholthin. It doesn't even feel cold."

She nuzzled his neck and began to spin them to help him stay warm. She pulled him closer.

"Well, now, that's a surprise," he said. "I didn't think I had it in me. Would you like to have it in you?" He giggled and her eyes sparkled as she purred intensely.

A moment later she pulled him inside her.

"*Shesmen'athuma*, Elinleo," she whispered into his ear.

"*Shesmen'athuma*, my precious Hiwholthin. I could not have loved anyone more than you. I could not have possibly been happier. I don't think I'm going to see your baby, I'm sorry to say. But maybe Abe and I can help keep an eye out for you."

He was too weak to push, so she rocked him back and forth inside her.

"Sweet Hiwholthin," he said and she vibrated with boundless love for him until he was finished.

"Elinleo," she whispered.

"I'm tired, dear love. I shall miss you so."

She whispered as softly as clouds. "Elinleo," she whispered. "*Shesmen'athuma. Gilpan-lostha.*" Soon-to-be-dead.

She held him close until he began to cool, their tears flowing into the River.

"*Shesmen'athuma. Eh'blemanthon. Shesmen'athuma foumou manessimuma. Foumou, foumou, foumou.*" Mate-lover. Safe friend.

Mate-lover destined to be food. *Foumou.* As it should be, as it should be, as it should be.

"*Elowinithin athuma*," she said to him. Love-care for the babies. You will nourish the babies.

"*Foumou*, Elinleo."

She pulled him under, toward the *thiflessa*.

A few hours later, Hiwholthin gave birth to a healthy Hlowenath daughter. Between nursing her, she slipped small pieces of him, softly chewed, into her baby's mouth. The wee one wriggled her toes and clung tightly to her mother's fur. As they slept, she dreamed that Leo swam into the *thiflessa* and held them both. She felt his warm body on hers and his brave breath on her neck.

Days passed. Her little one was too young to swim, but Hiwholthin splashed her little feet into the cold River daily. They purred back and forth. She felt Elinleo's spirit patrolling the River nearby. He did not speak but often popped his head up into the *thiflessa*, smiling happily, to check on them and leave food, tiny shells, and bits of shiny rocks.

On the fifth day, Leo's spirit was curled up near the waterway access. Hiwholthin rested a foot against his leg. He turned toward her, and gazed at the baby, his eyes suddenly wide.

Hiwholthin looked down to see her baby's *wessethia,* her secondary lids, slide open for the first time, revealing the dark brown fire of her kind.

Hiwholthin sighed happily and lifted her baby toward the ceiling of the *thiflessa*.

"Elowinithin *brerr Afleni*," she said. Elowinithin has become the Afleni.

Leo beamed. An apt name indeed. His spirit *shelossithis*—swam silently—to fetch more food.

Nine days later, Hiwholthin gave birth again. She had Seconded.

She had preserved the line.

She examined the newer baby, noting good fur a little curlier than his sister's, a tiny but familiar-looking penis. His hands were less webbed but considerably stronger, very dexterous. He touched her face again and again.

Winter days passed. Leo's bones rested on the Riverbed, save some finger bones which she had woven into her hair. The Second was as healthy as his sister. The babies were settled enough to stay in the *thiflessa* alone as she hunted for them. Leo was always nearby.

Still, Hiwholthin was concerned. The male's eyes were still closed. Too long. She fretted and cooed, purring at both the babies. But worried for Leo's kin.

It was evening, days later, when she entered the *thiflessa*, shook off the cold water, dropped fresh moss in the corner to dry, and laid food onto the floor. She looked at her babies, awash in love for them both.

As she turned to pick up the male, his *wessethia* slid open for the first time.

His eyes were blue.

Tears of joy splashed onto the floor of the *thiflessa*. She gathered him up, then lifted him to the ceiling.

"Elinleothon *brerr Alfeni*," she called to water, sky, and earth. Elinleothon has become the Afleni.

"Elinleothon," she purred at him. Son of Elinleo. She curled around them, Elowinithin and Elinleothon. The line would perdure.

"Elinleo," she purred. "Elinleo." Tears of loss. Tears of joy. Tears of life.

They slept until spring. In her dreams she felt Leo holding station nearby, whispering cuckoo songs to them all.

Chapter 14:

A Cuckoo's Splash
(Five Months Later)

"We told the nephew, Edward is his name, that his Uncle accidentally fell into the river and drowned. He knew Leo was very ill," Dr. Rob Schafhirt said to Cora Kowalski, the Bridge Operations Manager.

"How did he take it?"

Rob paused a moment and looked with kindness at the rapidly becoming teenage boy leaning over the bridge railing.

"He said that Leo told him that he'd be happy if one day the river carried him to the far side. The kid is happy. More like his Uncle Leo than his old man."

"So, what's with the cuckoo clock?" Cora asked.

"Ed has been very enigmatic about that. I don't really know.

"Leo told him to wait until the first full moon in April, bring the clock to the Bridgehouse, and let it sound twelve calls to the river. Leo's mind wasn't all that clear at the end, but the boy feels an obligation to him."

"Well, it's a little off the books, for sure, Doc. We're basically sneaking him into a Bridgehouse, secure infrastructure at night. Definitely against city policy. But if we get caught, I'll smooth things over, Leo style," she laughed confidently.

"Leo style? What's that?"

"I know how to wear my bosses out. Then they go away. Most of my job involves getting Bridge Operators out of trouble. I'm very good at my job. I help all these boneheads out. Some more than others. Leo was my favorite impossible Operator."

"Leo style," Rob smiled. "He really respected you, Cora."

"Shut up, Doctor. I promised myself I wouldn't cry at work. Now, look at me.

"Anyway, don't worry about it. If I have to, I'll buffalo the Director of Bridges with sass and bullshit until he gives up. Believe me, covering Bridge Operators' asses is a skill I've perfected. He's no challenge, but I don't want to burn up all my goodwill over a dead guy. "Wish Leo was still here so I could give him shit for drinking in the Bridgehouse. Again."

She looked at the river.

"You're going to have to stay next to the kid on the pitwalk though, Doc. For God's sake don't let him fall in."

Rob watched her suddenly turn away, wiping her eyes.

"If these Operators don't start cleaning these damn windows, I'm gonna kick their asses."

"Don't worry, Cora. I'll watch him closely. Ed's parents wanted nothing to do with this whole thing. But I would do anything for Leo."

"I'll wait up here and have a cigarette. Take your time. But not too long, okay?"

Ed and Rob walked down the spiral stairs to the pitwalk.

"I know the way, Doctor Rob. Uncle Leo sneaked me in there a lot last year. He said I should know what it looks like. But he said if I ever thought about becoming a Bridge Operator, he'd kick my ass."

"I'm not surprised by any of that. He's right about your job prospects. He'd definitely kick your ass. Have you ever thought about what you are going to be?"

Ed paused at the pit level door. "A research thanatology psychologist. I want to know where the mind goes when we die, Doctor Rob. Uncle Leo said the mind is like a cuckoo clock—it sings forever. He said Abe Lincoln told him that, but he was pretty whoo-whoo just before he disappeared.

"He's here in the river somewhere, Doctor Rob. He said the clock would give me the surprise of my life, just like it gave to him. I trust my uncle, but he was pretty wacky sometimes. I'm not so sure what's going to happen tonight."

Schafhirt looked at the river for a long time. "The mind is a helluva thing, Ed. Frankly, we don't know very much about it. We know even less about death. But if your Uncle suggested you do this, I'm sure it's because he loved you so much."

"Loves me, Dr. Rob. Present tense. He told me not to get confused about death. It's a door, not a wall, he said. He promised to keep talking to me as long as I would talk to him. So, I do. He's not here, but he's not gone. That's weird, hey? We talk together every day.

"One day, when I'm older, I'll know *exactly* how that works."

"Ed, that's the most beautiful thing I've ever heard. I loved him, too. Doggone it, I've been talking to him every day since he disappeared, seems like the only right thing to do. It feels like he's right there next to me, busting my chops like always.

"You should know that he has ordered me to seal his medical records until you complete your undergraduate degree. Then I am to release them to you. Did you know that? I think you are going to find that he's spot on about that door-not-a-wall thing.

Ed looked downriver, unknowingly toward the *thiflessa*.

"That will be a good day, Doctor Rob."

"What do you say, then, Ed? Ready to fire up the clock? Should I hold it for you? Or would it be best if I just let you alone?"

Ed paused to think. "It's OK if you stay, Doctor Rob. But I won't need any help. Uncle Leo showed me how to trigger the cuckoo. He put a special spring inside so that I could do it without needing any weights. He was a genius."

"Yes, he was. A little crazy, too."

"Probably," Ed said. "He told me that you would say that. And when you did, I was supposed to tell you 'It takes one to know one.'"

Schafhirt roared with laughter.

"Ed, your Uncle was the most amazing man I have ever known. I am so happy you were old enough to appreciate him. And I hope that you'll be kind enough to keep me in your life. That way, he'll always have his important people watching out for each other."

"That's what he wanted, Doctor Rob. He had it all figured out."

"So, let's get this show on the road, Ed. Cora is getting anxious."

"OK, Doctor Rob."

"Aw, hell. I need to take this call, Ed. It's the hospital. A Doctor's penance. Please, stay away from the rail. I'll be back in three minutes.

"This is Dr. Schafhirt. Yes? What are his vital signs?"

The pitwalk door closed behind him. Only moonglow, the amber drops from the streetlights above, and the pit level safety lights touched the river.

Edenkoben "Ed" Leonard Milhoan looked at the river, checked to make sure there was no way he could drop the precious clock into the river, and touched the small mother-of-pearl button tucked up in the eaves of the cuckoo's house.

The sound was beautiful. Ed looked at the river, feeling his Uncle close, a hint of his musky, Scotch-informed smell. His eyes washed over with tears.

On the sixth cuckoo, Hiwholthin crested the surface at Ed's feet. The two babies clung to her fur, staring at Ed, enchanted by the sound of the cuckoo.

Mouth agape, Ed pulled his sleeve across his eyes just as the clock called twelve.

"*Elineo'blemanthon!*" she said. Safe friend kin of Elineo. "*Elineo'blemanthon!*" Purring.

She held her boy baby up. "Elinleo. Elinleo."

Ed carefully put the clock onto the concrete pitwalk, well away from both river and pit, and knelt as close to her as he could.

"Elowinithin *brerr Afleni*," she said, holding the female-child up.

"Elinleothon *brerr Afleni*," she said, holding the male-child up.

Ed gasped. "He has my Uncle's eyes."

Hiwholthin understood, her own eyes brimming, purring even louder.

The door swung open. "Sorry for the emergency. Jesus Christ, Ed. You're really close to the water. You, OK?"

Hiwholthin and babies disappeared at the first sound.

Ed nodded, looking up. "I'm like my Uncle. I am always OK, Doctor Rob. This river is so beautiful. Just like Uncle Leo taught me. Beautiful and rich with surprises."

Rob knelt down next to him, resting a warm hand on his shoulder.

"I'll go run interference with Cora. Take your time, kid. I'll see you topside. Please close this door behind you.

"Don't forget the clock," he joked.

"Not a chance," Ed smiled.

A moment later, Hiwholthin crested again, the babies close enough to hold on, but clearly curious about him.

She splashed at him. Purring. Moving her eyes quickly from his, then to her babies, to potential threats, to him again.

"My name is Ed," he said. "Ed. My Uncle Leo told me about you. You're Hiwholthin!"

Hearing him speak her name, she purred joyously, the babies doing their best to emulate her, their eyes also fixed on him. She splashed at him again.

"Edwinleo!" She lifted the little ones closer to him.

"He has blue eyes, Hiwholthin," he said. "Like mine."

She smiled. "Elinleo." She pushed closer so the babies could touch him.

"Elowinithin. Elinleothon."

"He told me about you, Hiwholthin. He told me before he died. He told me after, too. I believed him, Hiwholthin. I always believed him."

"Edwinleo," she purred.

"I'll come back, Hiwholthin! I'll come back soon, OK?"

She looked at him, awash in love. He was one of hers, too.

"*Foumou*, Edwinleo. *Foumou*." As it should be.

She dove just as Doc called out from topside. "We should go soon, Ed!"

Edwinleo stared after her and her family. His family.

"I promise, Hiwholthin! Soon! I promise."

A Short Glossary of *Afleni* Words

Hiwholthin is a female of the Afleni race. Being primarily water beings, the language flows like the rivers her kind inhabit. It is a language spoken softly, as water sounds usually are. But it admits of intensity and passion, two qualities not often associated with faucet water but which perfectly accounts for natural flows. A language of few words, context and intention are entirely relevant to meaning. Have no worries about pronunciation. Once you've met your first *Afleni*, they will generously, maybe lovingly correct you.

The entries are in order of occurrence.

Thiflessa: Den, home, abode. A female becomes the *thiflessa* for her unborn babies.

Flissanthia: to be or become invisible in plain sight.

Elowinithin: the baby within.

Sha-sha: literally, just one. The unusual repetition of the word emphasizes singularity.

Eh'blemanthon: safe-friend, one-safe or one-who-is-safe; as a verb mate-lover.

Khahathontha: later-dangerous; as predators, *Afleni* encounter many dangerous beings but distinguish between those which are immediately dangerous and those which are not.

Manessimuna: food, prey.

Shessishess: to flee noisily, splashing or water-slapping.

Halawanthala: urgency

Thipthipen: the unique anatomy of *Afleni* females—having two uteri. The evolutionary benefit of this unusual pairing is not known at the time of this writing.

Shelossithis: to swim effortlessly, on the surface and underwater. The *Afleni* are air-dependent (gill-less) beings.

Afleni: the name of Hiwholthin's race of beings.

Elinleo: the *Afleni* pronunciation of the human name Leo. The Human words, especially proper names do not flow sufficiently for clear understanding.

Amelthr-amomn: arousing (esp. Sexually); interesting, appealing (esp. Food)

Shesmen'athuma: at its most basic, this term refers to sexual mating, including love, mate-love. More importantly, it is a word of consent to sexual contact of any kind. It must be voluntarily invoked by each partner prior to sexual contact and reaffirmed frequently during lovemaking. The primary benefit seems to be lovemaking as a relational, woven experience, not merely a sexual act or encounter. By human standards, the *Afleni* are highly sexualized. But they are never indiscriminate. Without active, shared, and ongoing consent, no ethical intercourse is possible.

Gilpanlostha: one who is soon-to-be-dead. This can be either observational or predictive.

Wha'hemoste athuma: root related to *shesmen'athuma*, this term is more deeply related to lovemaking—literally "I will kill for love." The *Afleni* are devoted.

Foumou: literally "must-to-be," it is often used as an intensifier of certitude; fated; destined.

Foumou shesmen'athuma: a must-to-be lover, destined-to-be lover.

Thipthipetha: the state of an *Afleni* female being with her second concurrent pregnancy.

moral activity applied to a one-loved.

Gilpan-khakthak: poisoned or otherwise inedible meat. The *Afleni* are hunter-gatherers. They do not eat carrion.

Shelosithis: a spirit being. The *Afleni* are in regular, interactive contact with a variety of spirits.

Don't miss out!

Visit the website below and you can sign up to receive emails whenever Paul E Shinkle publishes a new book. There's no charge and no obligation.

https://books2read.com/r/B-A-AQPWB-SZZZE

BOOKS 2 READ

Connecting independent readers to independent writers.

Did you love *Hiwholthin: A Supernatural Love*? Then you should read *23: Stories Short*[1] by Paul E Shinkle!

[2]

An exhausted neurosurgeon uses her power to see the future to help a worn-out waitress; The ghost of a suicide begs you to help him avoid hell by doing him just one favor; An uncle and his nephew, both philosophers, argue the merits of love over Scotch and pancakes; A photographer at a Santa shoot finds the real deal; A man leaves his workplace and walks into a mass shooting; does he run or render aid? A bookseller meets a customer with a particular way of loving books. 23: Stories Short is a compilation of stories and poems about regular people living extraordinary emotions; ones you thought only you have felt.

---

1. https://books2read.com/u/3kQENn

2. https://books2read.com/u/3kQENn

About the Author

Shinkle is a former firefighter, pastry chef, and teaching philosopher devoted to telling the stories of the bravest--or at least the most daring of us.

Hiwholthin is his 3rd book.